HOW TO USE YOUR LIGHTSABER

Your lightsaber toy is made up of two interlocking parts. Make sure the top and bottom parts are fully locked before you play with your toy. To light up your toy, move the switch on the handle to the right. Do not look into the light when your toy is ON. The handle also doubles as an image projector.

How to use your lightsaber as a projector:

- Twist and remove the green component from the handle of the lightsaber and set it aside.

- In this book, start with Disk 3 and slide the picture disk into the slot as shown.

- Pick a clear space on a light-colored wall or ceiling three to five feet away. The biggest images can be seen when the projector is five feet from the wall or ceiling.

- Turn the projector ON.*

- Turn the disk to the right as you read through the story. The numbers next to the text correspond to the numbers on the projected images. Use the focusing ring at the end of the image projector to focus the pictures.

- Change disks as indicated in the story.

*Remember to turn the switch to OFF when not in use.

Interlocking Notch

Focusing Ring

Disk

Slot for Disk

ON/OFF Switch

STAR WARS®
EPISODE V
THE EMPIRE STRIKES BACK

MOVIE THEATER
Storybook & Lightsaber Projector

Adapted by Benjamin Harper

studio fun

A READER'S DIGEST COMPANY

White Plains, New York • Montréal, Québec • Bath, United Kingdom

Deep in space, the Empire launched several probe droids toward different planets. They were looking for the new rebel base. Darth Vader's new mission was to find rebel leader, Luke Skywalker, who had destroyed the Death Star three years earlier.

One droid soared toward an icy planet called Hoth. Luke Skywalker saw the droid as it made impact. He told Han Solo he was going to investigate.

Luke was riding his tauntaun through the snow when a giant wampa attacked them! The monster dragged the unconscious Luke off to its den.

DISK 3

1

When Luke didn't report back from his rounds, Han Solo and the rebels became worried. Han went to look for his friend.

Luke regained consciousness in the icy cave and recovered his lightsaber in time to fight off the wampa. Luke ran out into the snow. A vision of Obi-Wan Kenobi told him to go to a planet called Dagobah and train with Jedi Master Yoda. Luke passed out just as Han came to rescue him.

The next day, the rebels picked up the probe droid's message to the Empire. They knew they had been discovered and planned the evacuation of their new base.

The rebels knew the
Empire would attack, so they
set up an energy shield. The Empire
had no choice but to land and fight on the ground.
Giant machines called AT-ATs marched toward the rebel base.

Luke and other rebel pilots manned snowspeeders and fought
the AT-ATs. They managed to tangle the walkers' legs with harpoons
and cables, making them crash. But some AT-ATs got through—and
one blew up the rebel shield generator so ships could land. Then
Darth Vader invaded the rebel base.

Luke Skywalker escaped
in his X-wing. Most rebels got
out in transport ships. Princess
Leia and Han Solo escaped in
the *Millennium Falcon*, but its
hyperdrive wasn't working! They
were chased through space.

3

Han and Leia were trapped in an asteroid belt above Hoth. Han thought Imperial troops wouldn't follow them into the dangerous asteroids, but he was mistaken. He hid his ship in a cave on a giant asteroid, so he could repair its hyperdrive.

Luke piloted his X-wing toward Dagobah. When he landed, his ship crashed into a swamp. Luke wasn't sure how he would find Jedi Master Yoda. The entire planet was a giant jungle! He and R2-D2 set up camp.

Luke was busy in his camp when a tiny green creature snuck
up on him. Luke didn't trust the creature but it said it knew where
Yoda was, so Luke followed it off into the jungle. When they arrived
at the creature's house, it revealed itself to be none other than
Master Yoda! The Jedi had played a trick to see how patient Luke
was. Luke promised he was ready to begin training.

DISK 4

1

Yoda taught Luke all about the Jedi and the Force. He also
warned about the evils of the dark side, and what it had done to
once-great Jedi like Darth Vader. Luke listened and learned.

In the giant asteroid, Han and Leia were busy fixing his ship when they discovered creatures outside. They went to investigate and discovered mynocks! The flying beasts were eating the ship's power cables. When Han went to clear them off, he accidentally blasted the floor of the cave. It shook. He fired again. It shook again. Something was wrong! They needed to leave immediately. As they flew out, the cave looked like it was collapsing—but it was no cave. A giant space slug had almost eaten them alive!

Aboard a Super Star Destroyer, Darth Vader ordered bounty hunters to find the *Millennium Falcon* and bring Han and Leia to him. As he was talking, Imperial Admiral Piett informed him that they had found the ship! It had come out of the asteroid field.

A Star Destroyer was chasing the *Falcon*. Han tried to jump into hyperspace, but his repairs hadn't worked. They were trapped! But Han had an idea. He turned the ship around and flew directly toward the Star Destroyer. He got so close that they no longer appeared in the Star Destroyer's scopes—as if the ship had disappeared! Han had attached the *Millennium Falcon* to the side of the Star Destroyer with a landing claw.

Angry that the *Millennium Falcon* had gotten away, Darth Vader ordered his fleet to disperse and search the galaxy. Then Han detached his ship and floated off into space, disguising his ship as space garbage. Unknown to Han, a bounty hunter named Boba Fett followed him and told the Empire where he was going!

Han flew to Cloud City, where he hoped his friend Lando Calrissian would help him repair the ship's hyperdrive. Lando greeted them and promised to help.

On Dagobah, Luke had a terrible vision. He saw his friends in a city in the clouds. They were in trouble! He decided he must help them. Yoda told him not to go, warning that he would fall to the dark side if he stopped training now. Obi-Wan appeared and told Luke he needed to stay. But Luke did not listen. He wanted to save his friends. He flew off toward Cloud City.

Darth Vader arrived in Cloud City before Han and Leia, and forced Lando to betray his friend Han Solo and help capture the rebels. He set a trap for them, preparing to use them as bait to bring Luke Skywalker to the Emperor.

Darth Vader also hatched a plan to freeze Luke Skywalker in carbonite to prevent him from struggling, but he wanted to test it first. He placed Han Solo in the carbon freeze chamber. Han was still alive, but frozen solid. Darth Vader gave Han Solo to Boba Fett, who took him to Jabba the Hutt to collect a reward.

3

Luke arrived at Cloud City. He saw Princess Leia and Chewbacca being led off by stormtroopers. Leia tried to warn Luke that he was falling into a trap, but it was too late. Darth Vader confronted Luke, and the two fought with lightsabers. Luke lost his hand in the battle but refused to give in. Darth Vader asked Luke to join him. Together, the Sith Lord told him, they could rule the galaxy!

Luke told Darth Vader that he knew the truth, that Darth Vader had turned to the dark side and had killed his father. And then Darth Vader revealed a great secret. *He* was Luke Skywalker's father. Luke couldn't believe it. He stopped struggling and dropped into an air duct to escape.

Leia, Chewbacca, and Lando managed to escape on the *Millennium Falcon*. They raced away from the city. The Empire was overtaking it.

Luke fell down an airshaft, which spat him out into the air below the floating city. He clung to an antenna dangling on the city's underbelly and called out to Leia, using the Force.

Leia heard Luke's cry and told Chewbacca to turn the *Millennium Falcon* around. They saw Luke barely hanging on to the antenna and maneuvered directly under him. Lando went out of the top hatch and grabbed Luke just as he was about to fall off. Lando brought Luke inside and Leia tended to his wounds.

Once again the hyperdrive was broken, but R2-D2 managed to fix it just as they were about to be captured. They zoomed off into hyperspace toward the rebel fleet!

The Rebel Alliance gathered in space. Aboard the medical frigate, a droid tended to Luke's wounds as Luke and Lando discussed a plan to rescue Han Solo from Jabba the Hutt on Tatooine.

As Luke, Leia, R2-D2, and C-3PO looked out into the stars, Lando and Chewbacca raced off to save their friend.

GENERAL SAFETY AND CARE

- Non-rechargeable batteries are not to be recharged.
- Different types of batteries or new and used batteries are not to be mixed.
- Batteries are to be inserted with the correct polarity.
- Exhausted batteries are to be removed from the toy.
- The supply terminals are not to be short-circuited.
- Do not mix old and new batteries.
- Do not mix alkaline, standard (carbon-zinc), or rechargeable (nickel-cadmium) batteries.
- Prevent the book and unit from getting wet and avoid exposure to excessively hot or cold temperatures.
- Rechargeable batteries are only to be charged under adult supervision.
- Rechargeable batteries are to be removed from the toy before being charged.
- Remove batteries when not in use or discharged.

BATTERY INFORMATION

To remove or insert replaceable batteries, remove the safety screw from battery compartment door. Lift and remove door. Take out and safely dispose of old batteries. Follow polarity diagram inside battery compartment to insert three new batteries of any of the following types: AG13 or equivalent. Alkaline batteries are recommended. Put battery compartment door back and secure safety screw. Do not use excess force or an improper type or size screwdriver.

CAUTION

To ensure proper safety and operation, battery replacement must always be done by an adult. Never let a child use this product unless battery door is secure. Batteries are small objects and could be ingested. Keep all batteries away from small children and immediately dispose of any used batteries safely. Projector is not a viewer. Do not look into the lens when light is on.